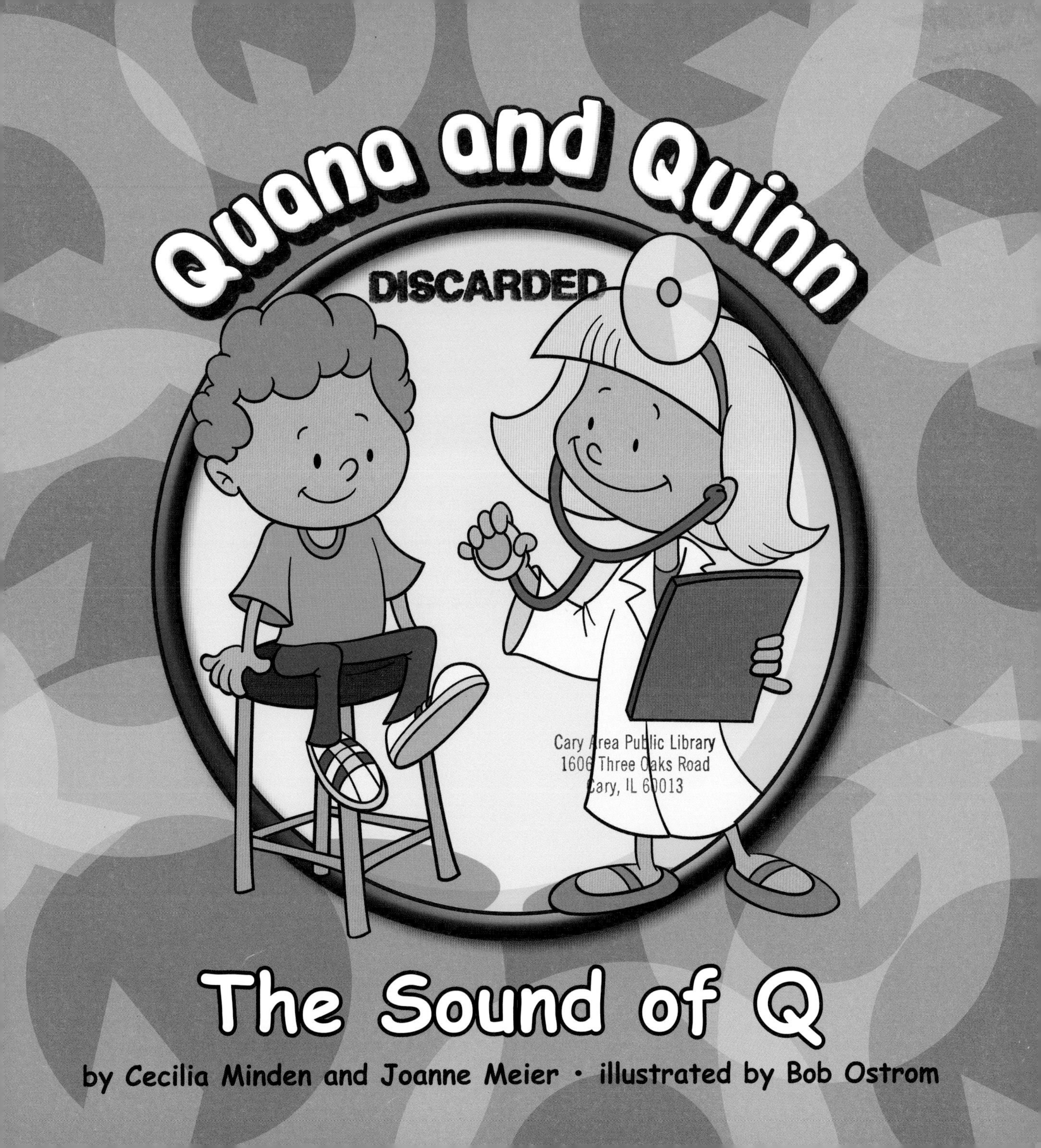
Quana and Quinn
The Sound of Q
by Cecilia Minden and Joanne Meier · illustrated by Bob Ostrom

Published by The Child's World®
1980 Lookout Drive
Mankato, MN 56003-1705
800-599-READ
www.childsworld.com

The Child's World®: Mary Berendes, Publishing Director
The Design Lab: Design and page production

Library of Congress Cataloging-in-Publication Data
Minden, Cecilia.
Quana and Quinn : the sound of Q / by Cecilia Minden and Joanne Meier ; illustrated by Bob Ostrom.
p. cm.
ISBN 978-1-60253-414-8 (library bound : alk. paper)
1. English language--Consonants--Juvenile literature. 2. English language--Phonetics--Juvenile literature. 3. Reading--Phonetic method--Juvenile literature. I. Meier, Joanne D. II. Ostrom, Bob. III. Title.
PE1159.M566 2010
[E]--dc22 2010005605

Printed in the United States of America in Mankato, MN.
July 2010
F11538

NOTE TO PARENTS AND EDUCATORS:

The Child's World® has created this series with the goal of exposing children to engaging stories and illustrations that assist in phonics development. The books in the series will help children learn the relationships between the letters of written language and the individual sounds of spoken language. This contact helps children learn to use these relationships to read and write words.

The books in this series follow a similar format. An introductory page, to be read by an adult, introduces the child to the phonics feature, or sound, that will be highlighted in the book. Read this page to the child, stressing the phonic feature. Help the student learn how to form the sound with her mouth. The story and engaging illustrations follow the introduction. At the end of the story, word lists categorize the feature words into their phonic elements.

Each book in this series has been carefully written to meet specific readability requirements. Close attention has been paid to elements such as word count, sentence length, and vocabulary. Readability formulas measure the ease with which the text can be read and understood. Each book in this series has been analyzed using the Spache readability formula.

Reading research suggests that systematic phonics instruction can greatly improve students' word recognition, spelling, and comprehension skills. This series assists in the teaching of phonics by providing students with important opportunities to apply their knowledge of phonics as they read words, sentences, and text.

This is the letter q.

In this book, you will read words that have the **q** sound as in: *queen, quick, quiet,* and *quilt.*

Quana likes to pretend.

Her little brother, Quinn,
does too.

Sometimes Quana is a queen. She wears a crown.

Quinn is the king.

He feels quite important!

Sometimes Quana is a doctor. She wants to care for Quinn.

Quinn is too quick.

He runs away!

It is time for bed.

It is time to be quiet.

Quana sleeps under a warm quilt. Quinn sleeps, too.

Quana and Quinn will be quiet and sleep. They will dream of new things to be.

Fun Facts

Many kings are married to queens, but one was married to six! Between 1509 and 1547, King Henry VIII of England was married to six different women. Four were from England, one was from Spain, and one was from Germany. Henry's daughter, Queen Elizabeth I, was the first queen to own a wristwatch. Elizabeth was the daughter of Henry's second wife, Queen Anne Boleyn.

You probably already know that sleeping under a quilt can be quite cozy, but did you know that some people think it brings good luck? Supposedly, any dreams you have the first night you sleep under a new quilt are likely to come true! Some quilters are also very careful not to break any thread as they work. They believe this could bring bad luck.

Activity

Designing Your Own Quilt

It might be difficult for you to make your own quilt without the help of an adult, but there's no reason you can't design one! With crayons or markers, divide a piece of paper into 25 squares. Decide what colors and shapes you would pick for each square. When you are finished, keep the design in a safe place for when you are ready to make your own quilt. Or perhaps a family member with experience making quilts would be willing to help you put one together based on your design!

To Learn More

Books

About the Sound of Q

Moncure, Jane Belk. *My "q" Sound Box®*. Mankato, MN: The Child's World, 2009.

About Queens

Buehner, Caralyn, and Mark Buehner (illustrator). *The Queen of Style*. New York: Dial Books for Young Readers, 2008.

Mannis, Celeste Davidson, and Bagram Ibatoulline (illustrator). *The Queen's Progress*. New York: Viking, 2003.

Paterson, John, Katherine Paterson, and Susan Jeffers (illustrator). *Blueberries for the Queen*. New York: HarperCollins, 2004.

About Quilts

Hopkinson, Deborah, and James Ransome (illustrator). *Sweet Clara and the Freedom Quilt*. New York: Dragonfly, 1995.

Johnston, Tony, and Tomie DePaola (illustrator). *The Quilt Story*. New York: Putnam & Grosset, 1996.

Polacco, Patricia. *The Keeping Quilt*. Orlando, Harcourt Brace, 1994.

Web Sites

Visit our home page for lots of links about the Sound of Q:

childsworld.com/links

Note to Parents, Teachers, and Librarians: We routinely check our Web links to make sure they're safe, active sites—so encourage your readers to check them out!

Q Feature Words

Proper Names

Quana
Quinn

Feature Words in Initial Position

queen
quick
quiet
quilt
quite

About the Authors

Cecilia Minden, PhD, is the former director of the Language and Literacy Program at the Harvard Graduate School of Education. She is now a reading consultant for school and library publications. She earned her PhD in reading education from the University of Virginia. Cecilia and her husband, Dave Cupp, live outside Chapel Hill, North Carolina. They enjoy sharing their love of reading with their grandchildren, Chelsea and Qadir.

Joanne Meier, PhD, has worked as an elementary school teacher, university professor, and researcher. She earned her BA in early childhood education from the University of South Carolina, and her MEd and PhD in education from the University of Virginia. She currently works as a literacy consultant for schools and private organizations. Joanne lives in Virginia with her husband Eric, daughters Kella and Erin, two cats, and a gerbil.

About the Illustrator

Bob Ostrom has been illustrating children's books for nearly twenty years. A graduate of the New England School of Art & Design at Suffolk University, Bob has worked for such companies as Disney, Nickelodeon, and Cartoon Network. He lives in North Carolina with his wife Melissa and three children, Will, Charlie, and Mae.

LANGUAGE ARTS

Learning About Poems

by Martha E. H. Rustad

Consulting Editor: Gail Saunders-Smith, PhD
Consultant: Kelly Boswell, educational consultant

CAPSTONE PRESS
a capstone imprint

Pebble Plus is published by Capstone Press,
1710 Roe Crest Drive, North Mankato, Minnesota 56003
www.capstonepub.com

Library of Congress Cataloging-in-Publication Data
Rustad, Martha E. H. (Martha Elizabeth Hillman), 1975–
Learning about poems / Martha E. H. Rustad.
pages cm—(Language arts)
Includes bibliographical references and index.
Includes webliography.
ISBN 978-1-4914-0580-2 (hb)—ISBN 978-1-4914-0614-4 (eb)—ISBN 978-1-4914-0648-9 (pb)
1. Poetics—Juvenile literature. 2. Poetry—Authorshp—Juvenile literature. 3. Children's poetry, American. I. Title.
PN1042.R86 2014
808.1—dc23 2014002015

Editorial Credits
Erika L. Shores, editor; Terri Poburka, designer; Charmaine Whitman, production specialist

Photo Credits
Shutterstock: Ahturner, 7, iofoto, 21, Karen Givens, 19 (dog), kesterhu, 19 (night sky), Legacy Images, 9, Levent Konuk, 11, luchschen, 17, Maxim Petrichuk, 5, Rob Marmion, 13, SNEHIT, 15, Szasz-Fabian Jozsef, cover (boy), topseller, cover (hot air balloon)

For Connie.—MEHR

Note to Parents and Teachers

The Language Arts set supports Common Core State Standards for Language Arts related to craft and structure, to text types and writing purpose, and to research for building and presenting knowledge. This book describes and illustrates poetry. The images support early readers in understanding the text. The repetition of words and phrases helps early readers learn new words. This book also introduces early readers to subject-specific vocabulary words, which are defined in the Glossary section. Early readers may need assistance to read some words and to use the Table of Contents, Glossary, Read More, Internet Sites, Critical Thinking Using the Common Core, and Index sections of the book.

Printed in the United States of America in North Mankato, Minnesota.
032014 008087CGF14

Table of Contents

What Is a Poem?

Poems connect words with senses and feelings. Words in a poem can make you feel warm and happy. They can make you feel silly or even sad.

Sunshine

by Laura Purdie Salas

Look for yellow
when you're weary

Smiling color
makes you cheery

Lemonade
in hot July

Flowers
reaching for the sky

Shining when
you need a lift

Nature's golden
brightest gift

A poet is someone who writes poems. Poets pick words carefully. In a poem, just a few words can tell us about a big idea.

Making Pancakes

by Laura Purdie Salas

pour the batter
Plip
Plop

brown both sides
Flip
Flop

spread the butter
Tip
Top

let the syrup
Drip
Drop

eat them all up
Don't
Stop!

Poem Parts

Poems are made up of lines and stanzas. A line is all the words in one row. A stanza is a group of lines.

line

Balloons

by Laura Purdie Salas

Brilliant bubbles dot the air
Bursting color everywhere

Drifting, floating, wandering high
Puffy rainbows fill the sky

stanza

Some poems use words
that rhyme, or sound alike.
In this poem, “rye,” “high,”
and “sky” rhyme.

Skyscraper Sandwich

by Laura Purdie Salas

I once built a sandwich on rye
Swiss cheese and bologna stretched high
It stood straight and tall
I did not let it fall
I stopped when my sandwich hit sky!

Rhythm is a pattern you hear
when you read words out loud.
Read the poem "Kick!" out loud.
Do you hear its steady rhythm?

Kick!

by Catherine Ipcizade

There once was a girl who could kick,
spent all of her days kicking sticks,
till she spotted a ball,
kicked it clear through a wall,
and began playing soccer right quick.

Some poems use one letter often.

This poem has a lot of S's.

Alliteration means using

the same letter often.

Snaking

by Laura Purdie Salas

Rivers
slither
through
like
snakes
stretching
in sun,
rippling
sleek
muscles

Some poems compare one thing to something else. This poem says snow covers things, just like a blanket does.

The First Snowfall

by Jennifer Fandel

Hard, cold
rains lighten to
white, shimmering crystals.
Like a blanket, the snow covers
us. *Hush.*

Kinds of Poems

Words are made of syllables. You hear a syllable as a loud or soft sound. In haikus and cinquains (SIN-kanes), each line has a certain number of syllables.

A haiku has
5 syllables,
7 syllables, and
5 syllables.

Persieds

by Martha E. H. Rustad

Shining stars up high,
Quiet night, you on my lap.
Meteors rain down.

No Need to Shower When Your Pet's a St. Bernard

for Brutus, by Blake Hoena

He shakes
his massive head,
and gobs of slobber fly,
showering the walls, the TV,
and me.

A cinquain has
2 syllables,
4 syllables,
6 syllables,
8 syllables, and
2 syllables.

Can you write an acrostic poem?

In acrostic poems, the first letter

in each line spells something.

Use the letters in your name.

You are a poet!

Music flows
Apple sliced
Retell a story
Kiss a nose
Under starry sky
Settle down

Glossary

acrostic—a poem that spells a word with the first letter of each line

alliteration—using several words that start with the same letter sound

cinquain—a poem that has a certain number of syllables in each line; the first line has two syllables, the second has four, the third has six, the fourth has eight, and the last line has two syllables

haiku—a poem that has a certain number of syllables in each line; the first and third lines have five syllables, and the second line has seven

line—all the words in one row of a poem

poet—a person who writes poems

rhyme—similar sounds in words

rhythm—a regular, repeated pattern heard when words are read aloud

stanza—a group of lines

syllable—one part of sound in a word

Read More

Loewen, Nancy. *Words, Wit, and Wonder: Writing Your Own Poem.* Writer's Toolbox. Minneapolis: Picture Window Books, 2009.

McCurry, Kristen. *Pick a Picture, Write a Poem!* Little Scribe. North Mankato, Minn.: Capstone Press, 2014.

Nesbitt, Kenn. *The Tighty Whitey Spider: And More Wacky Animal Poems I Totally Made Up.* Naperville, Ill.: Sourcebooks Jabberwocky, 2010.

Internet Sites

FactHound offers a safe, fun way to find Internet sites related to this book. All of the sites on FactHound have been researched by our staff.

Here's all you do:

Visit *www.facthound.com*

Type in this code: 9781491405802

Critical Thinking Using the Common Core

1. Some poems use alliteration. Describe what alliteration means. Try writing a poem that uses alliteration. (Craft and Structure)

2. Describe how you can tell if a poem is a haiku or a cinquain. (Key Ideas and Details)

Index

Word Count: 210 (main text)
Grade: 1
Early-Intervention Level: 18